BEWARE! WATERMELON MONSTER

Published in this edition by Willowisp Press, Inc.
401 E. Wilson Bridge Road, Worthington, Ohio 43085

Printed in the United States of America

10 9 8 7 6 5 4 3 2 1

ISBN 0-87406-295-0

BEWARE! WATERMELON MONSTER

Original text written and illustrated by Marta Koci

English text written by Jo Osborne

Marta Koci

Eating in the barn
at break of day,
two little pigs
run off to play.

Giggle, scurry,
wake up the cat.
Look in the shed.
What is that?

Something to play with?

Let's go see.

Shiny green balls,

what can they be?

Frog will tell them.

So will mice.

Watermelon! Watermelon!

Tastes so nice.

Nibble and splash,
juicy and sweet.
Pigs dive in for a
watermelon treat.

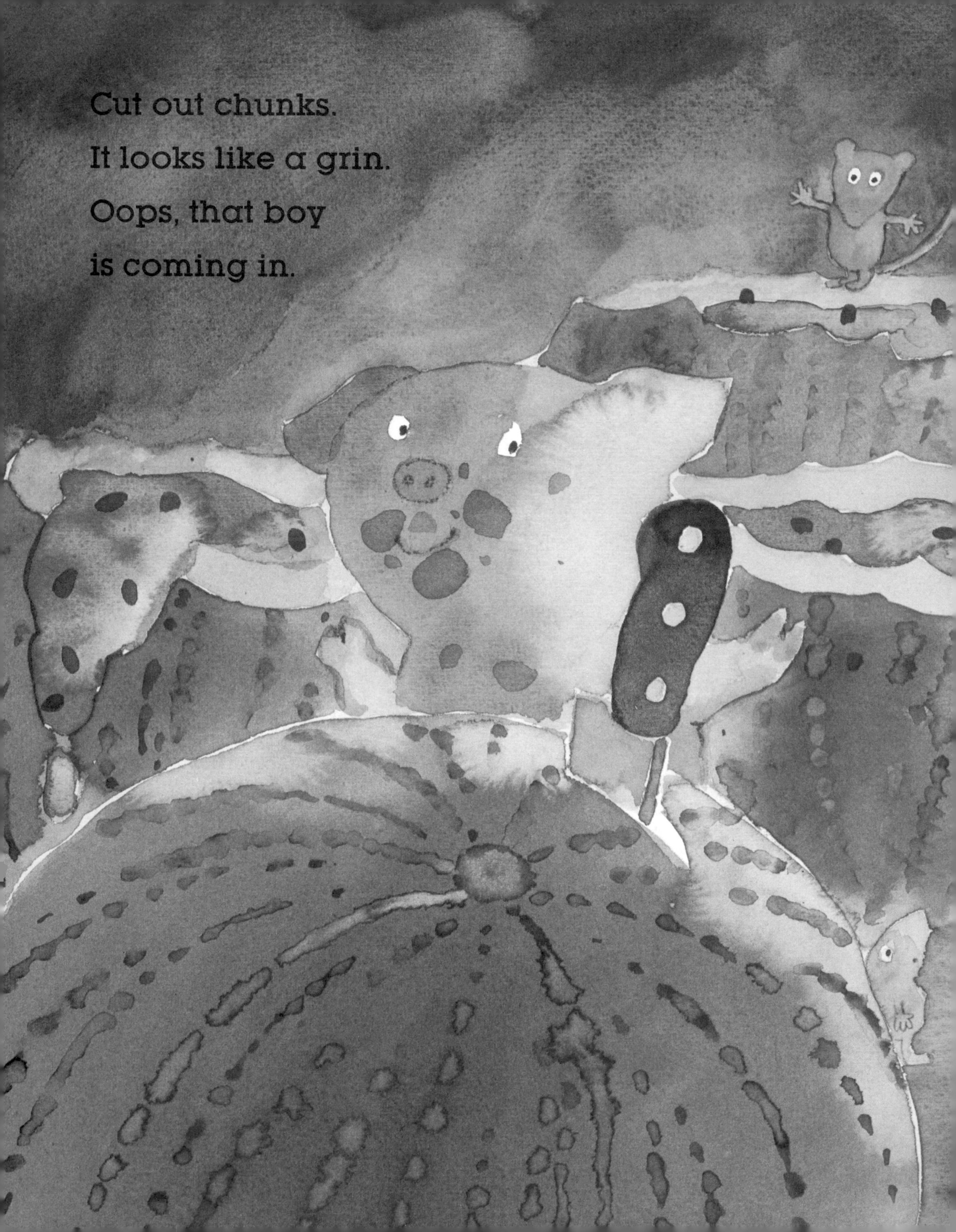

Cut out chunks.
It looks like a grin.
Oops, that boy
is coming in.

He'll catch us when
he comes inside.
Here's a blanket.
Quick, let's hide.

Over the head,
holler and roar.
Watermelon monster
runs out the door.

Monster yells,
"Hey, scaredy cat!"
Kitty runs.
Milk goes splat.

RE

Roaring, rushing,
this is fun.
Now the puppy's
on the run.

Can't see a thing.
Going to be a crash.
Here's the pond.
Monster goes splash.

Help! Help!

Monster disappears.

Help! Help!

Hope that someone hears.

Little boy rescued them.
Shout hooray
for watermelon monster,
watermelon day.